TWILIGHT QUEST

Laura Shenton

TWILIGHT QUEST

Laura Shenton

Iridescent Toad Publishing

*Extra special thanks to Christina Barfoot
for helping me bring this book to life.*

Chapter One

As the sun descended below the horizon, it cast an almost eerie glow over the town of Willowbrook. While most residents were preparing to settle down for a peaceful night's sleep, Cierra was wide awake. In the calm serenity of the twilight, she tugged at the cuffs of her black leather bodysuit, pulling them down over her wrists.

Hearing the clock tower nearby strike eight, Cierra's sharp gaze swept over her surroundings. From her vantage point on the high rooftop, she could see gas lamps flickering dimly, providing pools of warm light that danced upon the cobblestones. She had always preferred to work when it was just light enough in the sky to see the streets below, but dark enough that she was completely shrouded in her position on the rooftops.

All was quiet, the summer night air heavy with the scent of damp earth and distant chimneys. The rhythmic clatter of horse-drawn carriages had long left the streets, the soundscape now punctuated only by the distant cry of an occasionally-present nocturnal creature.

Willowbrook had been relatively civil for the last few weeks. Nothing in the air told Cierra that tonight would be any different. Confident that there was nothing out there that required her immediate attention, she tossed her long moon-white hair over her shoulders, continuing to dutifully observe the streets below with the predatory focus of a street cat on the hunt for mice.

Cierra had always gone against the typical conventions of assassins when it came to finding assignments. In not wishing to attract scorned lovers or malicious individuals seeking revenge, she never took on clients. Instead, she viewed herself as a protector of the night, and of all who stepped through her domain. It meant that her income remained sporadic, but in any situation that had required her skills, she had never had any trouble demanding payment after the fact.

Satisfied that all was well, but always mindful that she couldn't afford to blow her cover, Cierra moved strategically away from her lookout point. As she darted over a patch of loose tiling, her foot slipped momentarily, but she was quick to regain her balance, accustomed to the slanted surfaces and the constant risk of falling. She knew how to distribute her weight to maintain stability. Skilfully navigating the gaps between the tall buildings, she relied on her agility, certain that she could get across. She moved with the fluid grace of a seasoned professional, her steps sure-footed despite the vertiginous heights.

Finally, she reached the roof adjacent to the building of her lodgings. With a final leap, she landed on the familiar ledge outside her bedroom window, her heart pounding with the exhilaration of the journey. With ease, she slipped through the open window, her movements fluid and silent as she entered the familiar confines of home.

Leaving her bedroom behind, Cierra walked

through the small hallway of the third-floor home. With richly-patterned paper adorning the walls, it exuded a timeless elegance, despite being a little shabby in its overall condition.

Entering the living area, Cierra spotted Violet, who was kneeling over a small table strewn with an assortment of flowers.

Dressed in a simple floral-print dress, Violet moved with grace and poise, her hands deftly weaving an intricate bouquet destined for market tomorrow. Pale and freckled, she had long strawberry-blonde hair that she had tied back with a pretty ribbon, keeping her free of distractions while she worked. The scent of the freshly-cut blooms lingered in the air, serving to remind Cierra that simple pleasures could be found amidst the intensity of her nocturnal existence.

"Violet," she said, completely unsurprised that her friend was still working. "You should be asleep. Don't you have an early start tomorrow?"

"Well, maybe," said Violet, giving a casual shrug as she handed a folded piece of paper to Cierra. "This came for you."

Observing the piece of paper in her hands, Cierra noticed that it was slightly creased, but otherwise unblemished. She flipped it over and saw her name in scribbled handwriting, causing her to blink in surprise.

"Who knows I live here?"

"I wouldn't have a clue," Violet said casually. "But it seems that you've caught the attention of someone."

"What?!" Cierra exclaimed, a look of horror spreading across her face. "Did you..."

"No," Violet replied, exasperated at having been asked the same question hundreds of times before. "I haven't told anyone that you live here with me. Nobody at the market, not the landlady, *nobody*."

Cierra nodded, and looked back down at the paper that was clearly a letter for her. She didn't even know if it would be wise to open it. Whoever it was, knew her – or at least, knew *of* her. She wasn't sure which would be worse. What could the contents be? She doubted it would be friendly.

"Right," Violet said tactfully. "I'll leave you to it. I'm going to bed."

She offered Cierra a sympathetic smile before turning around and retreating down the hallway. Upon hearing Violet's bedroom door click shut, Cierra slumped down on the sofa, still clutching the letter.

Although the letter wasn't sealed, Cierra trusted that Violet hadn't read it. Despite Violet's occasional naivety and lack of knowledge about Cierra's occupation, their relationship was founded on trust and mutual respect.

Flipping open the folded page, Cierra noticed straight away that the handwritten message within was fairly short:

Cierra,

We share a common goal. Meet me on the roof of the Cairn's residence at twilight. I'll explain everything then.

Cierra was astounded. The stranger who had declined to reveal their identity knew her name and where she lived. The message had the traits of something written from one assassin to another; nobody else would seek to meet on a rooftop.

Cierra had only ever met one fellow assassin before – and that had been her trainer, who she'd lost contact with years ago. Never when patrolling Willowbrook had she ever bumped into anyone else on a similar mission.

She bit down on her bottom lip. Did she even dare go to meet the stranger in question? Equally though, it could be a dangerous decision to ignore the letter entirely.

Cierra wished that the sender had offered more information, but knew that if it truly was another assassin, it would have been foolish of them to do so.

Deciding not to spend the entire night in the living room, Cierra wandered down the hall and into her bedroom. There was a simple bed and nightstand in the corner, with an ornate wardrobe placed at the end. The small blue rug on the floor was obstructed by a large bookshelf that had been placed on top of it. She would be forever grateful to Violet for having allowed her to stay here.

Letter still in hand, Cierra laid down on her bed and flicked on the lamp on the nightstand. She read the message again, and then several times more to check whether it perhaps contained any secrets.

But no. There was nothing to suggest that the message had anything to convey other than what was explicitly on the page. No code, no markings.

Taking a deep breath, Cierra made her decision. She would go to meet this other assassin. She knew that if she didn't, she would always have to live with the thought that someone else out there could be in grave danger.

Aware that the message could be an invitation into an ambush, she patted the two blades that she kept in sheaths around her legs. Perfectly concealed beneath the length of her upper body armour, at a glance, to the untrained eye, it looked as though there was nothing there.

Though she had confidence in her trusty blades, she felt strongly that she would need to take every possible measure in preparation for a meeting of such an unusual nature.

Chapter Two

By the time Cierra woke up, the sun was already high up in the sky. It beamed down on her through the large window overlooking her bed. Still in her outfit from the night before, she blinked the sleep out of her eyes. The nocturnal nature of the hours she kept was such that it wasn't unusual for her to sleep so late into the day. All the same though, she needed to get moving.

She quickly changed into a smart combination of dark jeans and a vest, adding a long black cardigan that barely kept her sheathed blades concealed. As she caught sight of the letter on the nightstand, she wished it had never arrived in the first place.

Stepping out of her bedroom, she saw that Violet had only just arrived home. Wearing a casual floral-print dress with her hair tied up,

Violet held the handle of a wicker basket filled with several bouquets of fresh flowers.

"Good, you're awake," Violet said as she walked into the kitchen area and started to place her items onto the worktop. "I was hoping that we could... Do you really have to wear those blades at home?! It makes me nervous. It's like you're expecting a fight or something."

"I just want to stay armed until I figure out what's going on. It's for our safety."

Anxious that an assassin knew where she lived, Cierra wasn't prepared to take the risk of being unarmed. She had already promised herself that after the meeting tonight, she would return to her previously agreed-upon rule with Violet that there was to be no weapon-wearing at home.

"Ok," Violet said hesitantly, seeming resigned to the idea that Cierra had her reasons. "Well, I was hoping you'd help me again – these bouquets don't make themselves."

"Of course," Cierra replied graciously.

The corner of her mouth twitched upwards to form a smile. Although she couldn't afford to let her guard down, she was almost grateful for the distraction.

"It's just that you've got such a good eye for colour," said Violet. "Besides, the more bouquets I can take with me to market, the more sales I can make."

Cierra sauntered over to the worktop, examining the beautiful flowers and streams of pretty ribbons. Pleased to see that everything she needed was there, she began to work.

"You don't have to do it right now," Violet told her, "just within the next couple of days."

"I'm free now," Cierra said, waving her hand dismissively. "What else am I going to do?"

Violet smiled empathetically and grabbed some of the other items from her basket: a couple of apples, some bread, and a block of cheese.

"Have you eaten yet?" she asked.

Cierra shook her head.

"I'll make you something."

Cierra sat down on the wooden stool at the worktop and began to get organised. Violet handed her the scissors to cut the stems.

As they both worked, Violet talked about her day. She always woke up early to head to market. She had spent the morning there.

Appearing satisfied that the cheese sandwiches and slices of apple were just right, Violet put the plate down in front of Cierra.

"Thanks," said Cierra, tucking in with enthusiasm.

"So..." said Violet. "I hope you're not upset about that letter that came for you last night."

Cierra considered her options. She knew that Violet was genuinely concerned and didn't wish to pry. Violet was a good friend and cared deeply about Cierra. Cierra had been living rent-free with Violet for quite some time.

Deciding that at the absolute minimum, she needed to offer Violet some reassurance, Cierra finally spoke.

"Someone wants to meet me. I don't know what they want."

"Oh," Violet uttered. "Are you going to go?"

"Yes," said Cierra. "I'll be ok. You don't need to worry."

Violet didn't know the details, and Cierra wanted to keep it that way.

Violet was quiet for a while as she worked on a bouquet, leaving Cierra to eat in peace. Finally though, evidently still worried, she plucked up the courage to ask another question.

"How do they know where you live?"

"I don't know," Cierra admitted. "I'm hoping to figure that out when I meet them. I can take care of myself, I promise. If you're worried about our safety, don't be."

It still unnerved Cierra that someone had been able to figure out her home address. She had already decided that she was going to interrogate an explanation out of the other assassin – if only to be certain that others wouldn't have the same opportunity to get their hands on the same information.

Violet inhaled a deep breath and then let it out slowly. Cierra noticed that there were deep bags under her eyes. She looked exhausted.

"I know you can take care of us," Violet said. "I've never doubted that. But... I don't know... I guess what I'm trying to say is, be careful."

"I will," said Cierra before nodding her head in the direction of the hallway. "Now go and get some sleep. You deserve a rest."

Cierra, acutely aware that Violet didn't have an easy life, watched as the young woman sighed and made her way down the hall. With no family or partner to rely on, Violet worked long hours and barely earned enough to make ends meet. Cierra often wondered how Violet coped, but they had an unspoken agreement not to pry too deeply into each other's lives. Violet was unaware of the specifics of Cierra's occupation, but appreciated her companionship nonetheless.

Even so, it bothered Cierra to know that her closest friend seemed to carry a lot of weight on her shoulders.

Chapter Three

Having been determined to get there early to scout the area, Cierra found herself on the rooftops almost an hour before twilight. Still unsure of the person who had sent her the letter, she reasoned that it was best to arrive first.

Traversing across the many rooftops in the vicinity, she circled the area twice in large, stealth-fuelled movements before finally perching on a ledge slightly higher than the Cairn's residence. Should the other assassin turn out to be bad news, she would need to have the upper hand.

Remaining crouched in the space between two chimneys, she double-checked her weapons. Her blades were in their sheaths, strapped to the tops of her thighs and invisible to others.

At the arrival of twilight, she spotted a dark figure moving towards the meeting point. It didn't seem that they were trying to hide. In fact, it was as though they wanted to be seen.

As the figure drew closer, their precise movements causing their long dark hair to billow out in waves behind them, it became clear to Cierra that they were female. The woman hopped from rooftop to rooftop in a way that only an assassin could, slivers of light hitting her pale skin, contrasting against her black leather bodysuit.

Pausing at the designated location, the woman didn't seem concerned that she hadn't yet spotted Cierra. Instead of looking around nervously, she sat patiently, waiting in the diminishing sunlight. She seemed so calm and casual in her body language that it was just what Cierra needed to be convinced that it was safe to proceed.

Moving with the silent grace of a cat unafraid to risk its nine lives, Cierra advanced, preparing to confront the woman.

"I'm pleasantly surprised you've shown up," the woman said without turning around, having already sensed Cierra's presence. "I wasn't sure if you would."

"Who are you?" Cierra asked, stepping around to face the woman. "How do you know where I live?"

The woman stood up, and spoke with confidence.

"I'm Taryn," she said. "I haven't been in this town for very long, and I don't plan on sticking around. I noticed you a few nights ago, and followed you back home. I apologise for the style of my approach, but I figured that it was the only way of being able to talk to you."

"Why?" Cierra demanded. "What do you want?"

"Before I tell you that, I need you to trust me," said Taryn, raising an eyebrow as her gaze fell to where she sensed Cierra had weapons. "I don't think we're quite there yet though."

Taryn was right. Cierra didn't trust her.

"I'm completely unarmed, by the way," Taryn

said. "You can check if you don't believe me. It does feel a bit odd to be without weapons, but I figured that if it came to it, you'd be more than capable of fighting for both of us tonight."

Taken aback by the presumptuous comment, Cierra scanned Taryn's body with narrowed eyes. Indeed, there was no obvious sign of any weapons.

Perhaps Taryn is telling the truth.

"Alright," Cierra said, raising her gaze to meet Taryn's. "I'm willing to listen. What do you want from me?"

"Thank you," said Taryn. "The first thing you need to know about me is that I hunt mutants. Of course, although some of them look obvious in their identity, there are those who look humanlike. That aside, they all drink human blood and will stop at nothing to get it. It is, after all, their life source."

Having had to fight a few mutants before, Cierra was familiar with them. Although they were typically grotesque in their nature, a single mutant had never been a match for her twin blades.

"I've taken on a few mutants in my time," she said, now satisfied that she and Taryn seemed to be on the same page.

"Good," said Taryn. "Recently, I have had to deal with quite a few of them. I have reason to believe that there's a particularly unpleasant one operating here in Willowbrook."

"I doubt that very much," said Cierra, slightly annoyed. "I'd know if there was a mutant causing trouble."

"Lady Blanch is adept at keeping below the radar," Taryn said, her hands resting confidently on her hips. "As I said, I need you to trust me."

"Lady Blanch?!" Cierra exclaimed. "I've seen her many times before. She seems completely normal – well, as normal as someone can be, considering how rich and powerful she is!"

"I can prove it to you," Taryn insisted. "Follow me."

As Taryn turned away and began racing for the neighbouring rooftops, Cierra bit down on her lip. Trust had never come easily to her. Not only was it in her nature to suspect everyone; it was essential for her survival.

Confident in the weaponry on her person, however, she sighed and decided to follow along after Taryn. As the assassin in front of her expertly jumped across the gaps between each rooftop, it felt as though the two of them were doing an elusive dance, communicating through their movements.

Finally, Taryn came to a halt, but they hadn't yet reached the edge of town where Cierra knew Lady Blanch's manor was. Instead, they were near a grand shop building – a bakery, of all places. Although Cierra had never stepped foot inside, she'd had her eye on the location for a while due to how people would often come and go from it at such unusual hours.

In the still of the night, only the moon and the streetlamps below illuminated the area. Beneath one particular streetlamp was a gold-plated carriage with two muscular white horses standing obediently. In the driver's seat, a man sat patiently waiting.

Her curiosity piqued, Cierra silently crouched down beside Taryn, who passed her a pair of binoculars.

"Use these," Taryn said in a low voice. "Be sure to keep an eye on the mouth of the woman who's about to step out. You'll see why in a moment."

Despite the 'closed' sign in the bakery window, the front door opened, and out stepped Lady Blanch. The tall woman's skin was pale to the point of appearing slightly ashen. Her dark hair was brushed upwards to sit voluminously beneath a large-brimmed hat. As she walked nonchalantly across the cobblestones, she pulled something out of the pocket of her long fur coat. It was a pipe. She stuffed it with tobacco before placing it in her mouth.

The elegantly-dressed woman then deftly lit a match to ignite the tobacco in her pipe. As she took a long, leisurely drag, tendrils of smoke curled around her slender fingers. Each of her movements exuded a regal poise.

As Lady Blanch milled around, talking quietly to the entourage of compliantly militant men around her, Cierra watched the whole scene through the binoculars, specifically paying attention to the woman's mouth. Suddenly, she saw it: a glint of crimson, a subtle-but-undeniable blemish, stark against smoke-stained teeth. It was a small detail that could easily be overlooked amidst the grandeur of the moment, but to Cierra, it was a revelation.

Blood! She's been drinking blood!

Horrified, Cierra shuddered. All of her doubts had been erased to be replaced by a chilling certainty: Lady Blanch was indeed a mutant.

Several men strode out from the bakery. At first, Cierra wasn't quite sure what she was witnessing. But then, she noticed that one man in particular was trembling, reluctance in his movements as he walked forward. Adjusting the binoculars, her pulse quickened as she realised that there was a gag in his mouth and his hands had been tied behind his back. When the group reached the carriage, the man faltered and shook his head frantically, as though pleading for mercy. Despite this, two of the men behind him gave him a hard shove, causing their victim to fall forward into the carriage before climbing in themselves.

Giving a nod of approval, Lady Blanch gracefully climbed up onto the seat beside the driver before giving the signal for them to leave.

The horses began to move and the carriage rolled down the street. Just as Cierra was about to move in order to follow the suspicious troop, she felt Taryn's hand wrap around her wrist in a strong grip.

"We should go after them," Cierra whispered urgently. "They have that man hostage. We have to help. From what we've just seen, it's clear that Lady Blanch is a mutant. He will be in grave danger."

Cierra winced as she pictured the domineering woman overpowering the poor man; with crimson-stained lips, she would surely drain him of his blood – every last drop.

"No," Taryn whispered, her tone laced with frustration. "Not yet. It's complicated. We need to keep a low profile for now."

Cierra frowned. She didn't like the thought of not going after the carriage, but she also sensed that Taryn was right. Moreover, it bothered her that it had taken another assassin to bring her attention to what had been happening in Willowbrook.

"Tell me everything you know," Cierra insisted.

"I've dealt with many mutants before," Taryn said. "I caught wind of this one from a few towns over. I didn't know much, only that a woman was running a large operation. I've been tracking it for a while, and when everything pointed towards Lady Blanch, I knew that it was time to reach out for assistance. The woman has a lot of acquaintances; I'm not sure if they are mutants, or simply ordinary people who are indebted to her in some way. It could be a combination of both. Either way, the sheer scale of her operation is such that I can't take it on alone."

Although it was a lot for Cierra to take in, she had a feeling in her gut that Taryn's explanation and motives were genuine. Besides, it wasn't every day that an assassin decided to out themselves to another.

"Count me in," Cierra finally said. "I sense that I can trust you."

"Thank you," said Taryn, relief evident in her smile.

"Ok," Cierra said. "The first thing we need to do is find out more about Lady Blanch. There's still a lot we don't know about her – we need to know what we're up against in terms of how powerful she is, and in terms of how many people she's got under her thumb. We mustn't underestimate anything at this stage."

"I agree," said Taryn. "My thoughts are that our next aim should be to gain entry into her manor. Based on how long she's been able to operate unnoticed, she must have everything under lock and key. I should hope that if you can cause a distraction, I could slip inside to start unearthing some vital information."

"Hmm..." Cierra mused. "I think we should hold back a bit first though. Although there could be innocent people in danger, and time is of the essence in that regard, we should watch from a distance for a good while yet – just until we can be certain of what we're dealing with."

"Good idea," said Taryn, bowing her head gratefully. "I'm glad to have you working with me on this."

Chapter Four

Crouched down low on a rooftop, despite how the insulated leather of her outfit served to protect her from the chill in the air, a shiver trailed down Cierra's spine. Amongst the anticipation of what was to come, her feelings were a blend of excitement and hesitation.

It would soon be twilight, which would see her meeting up with Taryn again. In their efforts to figure out what was going on with Lady Blanch and her entourage, they would need to get information from the bottom, and work their way to the top. Other than that, Cierra had no idea what to expect of Taryn in terms of how she would choose to approach the situation. She knew though, that because Taryn seemed to have a better understanding of the whole thing, she needed to be willing to take a back seat, at least for now.

As daylight faded and gave way to twilight, Taryn finally appeared, her black leather bodysuit snug against her lithe form.

"Follow me," she said.

Respectful and admiring of how Taryn wasn't willing to lose time in exchanging pleasantries, Cierra nodded in compliance. She had to trust that the other assassin could be followed.

As Taryn darted across the rooftops ahead of Cierra, there was a speed and accuracy in her steps; she moved quickly, but not hastily. Impressed, Cierra managed to keep up the pace without faltering.

Finally, Taryn came to a halt on one of the roofs in a part of the town that Cierra recognised as the more wealthy side. As well as a bank, there were a few shops and residential properties, all opulent and in pristine condition. The glow of gas lamps illuminated the cobblestone streets below, casting long shadows.

"We have to hurry," Taryn said in a low murmur as she turned to address Cierra. "The guard rotation will be happening soon."

"We're breaking into the bank?!" Cierra whispered, her brows flicking up in surprise as she studied Taryn incredulously.

"Only because we have to," Taryn confirmed, craning her neck to keep an eye on the guard below.

As Cierra looked down to do her own observations, she took in the sight of the guard. He was pacing back and forth across the cobblestones, a loaded crossbow held tightly in his hands.

"The bank holds all of Lady Blanch's financial records," Taryn whispered. "If we can get hold of them, we'll be able to find out what properties she has, and hopefully, who's indebted to her."

Taryn's reasoning made sense to Cierra, but still she could see a hole in the plan.

"How can we be sure that Lady Blanch is doing everything legally?" she asked. "What if her records reveal only a fraction of what she's really up to?"

"Fair point," said Taryn. "I've got a hunch that we're starting off along the right lines though. I could be wrong, but nothing ventured: nothing gained."

Cierra nodded in agreement. She couldn't fault Taryn's logic.

"I assume you're armed," she said to Taryn.

Taryn simply smiled, a confident glint in her eyes. Though none of her weapons were visible on the outside of her outfit, her expression made it clear that they were present, concealed and readily accessible.

With the guard below standing in an open space, Cierra knew that she and Taryn wouldn't be able to jump across to the bank's roof until it was time for him to swap places with a colleague.

Despite her considerable skill and experience, Cierra couldn't shake the nagging sense of nervousness that gripped her. She had never broken into such an important building before. It had always been homes and smaller businesses, and even they hadn't been frequent. She had always preferred to do her work on the streets and in alleys, where her presence was harder to detect.

Taryn, however, didn't seem phased by what they were about to do. She waited calmly, never once taking her eyes off the guard.

Finally, it happened. The guard stepped up to the bank door, produced a key, and then slipped inside. Taking this as her cue, Taryn sprang into action. Immediately, Cierra followed quickly behind her. They jumped the gap between several roofs, working their way around until they reached the roof of the bank. Then, after checking that the coast was clear, they slid down the drainpipe to the side door of the building.

Expecting the door to be locked, Cierra pulled a pair of lock picks from one of her many hidden pockets. She got to work, and within a matter of seconds, the lock clicked open, allowing them to stealthily enter the bank.

Once they were inside, Taryn quietly shut the door behind them. Like ghosts, they then melted into the shadows, their movements swift and soundless.

Cierra's pulse quickened as she scanned the dimly lit space, her keen eyes catching the subtle shift of movement that betrayed the presence of a guard several hundred metres away. Amidst the tension that hung thick in the air, she remained composed, her movements fluid and deliberate as she and Taryn edged themselves into an empty side room.

"I've been researching this place for a while," Taryn whispered into Cierra's ear. "I know where the records are kept."

Once the coast was clear, with Taryn taking the lead, the two assassins slunk expertly along the narrow corridors, their lithe silhouettes barely blurs in the darkness.

As they reached the heavy oak door of their target room, undeterred, Cierra withdrew her lock picks again. With practiced ease, her fingers moved deftly as she manipulated the intricate mechanism of the lock before her.

Soon enough, the door swung quietly open to reveal rows upon rows of filing cabinets, all labelled in alphabetical order.

Taking a box of matches from a pocket inside her bodysuit, Taryn struck one, holding it precisely between her finger and thumb to serve as a small candle.

"We're looking for properties filed under 'Blanch', aren't we?" Cierra asked in a low whisper.

"That's right," Taryn quietly confirmed as she began searching a shelf at the opposite end of the small room.

Cierra's slender fingers trailed along the aged spines of leather-bound ledgers, her eyes scanning the meticulously handwritten labels that adorned each shelf. In the dim glow of her own single matchstick flame, the musty scent of old parchment filled the air, mingling with the faint aroma of wood and dust.

With a furrowed brow, she focused her attention on the 'B' section, her gaze sweeping over the abundance of catalogued records. Yet, despite her efforts, the name they sought remained elusive.

Undeterred, she kept looking, delving into the forgotten recesses of the older cabinets, and then older still, until finally, she came to a drawer labelled with the surname Blanch. She then looked down at the shelf below, and noticed another drawer with the same label. Beneath that one, there was another. She couldn't believe it: three drawers, solely dedicated to one woman.

She grabbed the bottommost cabinet and

pulled it open. It had been crammed with endless stacks of paper. As she sifted through them, she discovered that many were transactions dating back to decades ago.

Having spotted the drawers dedicated to their target, Taryn pulled open the one on top and began to browse through it.

"According to this relatively recent document," she murmured close to Cierra's ear, "it seems that Lady Blanch currently owns thirty-four lots in Willowbrook."

As Taryn quietly reeled off the names of some of the properties, Cierra's mind raced with a mixture of disbelief and consternation. Each one listed was like a dagger piercing the veil of her assumptions, revealing the impressive assets of their target. It worried Cierra to think that despite the scale of Lady Blanch's immense wealth and influence in the town, she had failed to recognise the woman as a mutant.

A heavy weight settled in the pit of Cierra's stomach, a stone of guilt and regret. She felt as though she had failed in her duty to protect the innocent, to safeguard the vulnerable from the machinations of those who sought to exploit them.

"Hey, Cierra," Taryn said quietly. "It says here that the Riverwood building is one of Lady Blanch's properties. That's where you live!"

"What?!" Cierra exclaimed, jerking her head up to meet Taryn's gaze. "That place is nothing to do with Lady Blanch! I would know about it if that was the case!"

Taryn struck another match for them to share the light from, and then passed the piece of paper down to Cierra, who grabbed it urgently.

Since when has Lady Blanch owned the building?

"At least with everything we've found here tonight," said Taryn, "we can be confident that in doing things via the bank, Lady Blanch takes an official approach to doing business. Potentially, the name of everyone who owes her money could be listed here."

Cierra was no longer paying attention to the bigger picture. She was too busy scanning the paper in her hand, looking for one name only: a name that could change everything.

Surely enough, just as Cierra had feared, there was the name: Violet Carter. Next to Violet's name, printed neatly in black ink, was a substantial amount of money that she owed: two-thousand pounds. Shocked at the stark clarity of the information on the page before her, Cierra's heart nearly stopped dead in her chest.

"Violet..." she whispered in fear, the words practically tumbling from her mouth.

"I don't mean to push," said Taryn, "but we can't stay here and study the details of every document. We need to leave."

With a nod of agreement, Cierra placed the page back into the drawer. She nearly groaned. Although they had gained some insight into the scale of Lady Blanch's operation, they were no closer to solving anything specific.

"I'll do more tracking tonight," Taryn muttered. "Shall we meet up again tomorrow?"

"I'm coming along with you," Cierra whispered instantly.

Chapter Five

When Cierra returned home in the small hours of the morning, Violet had already left for work. Considering all the questions that Cierra wanted to ask, Violet had probably, without having realised it, done herself a favour.

Why is Violet in debt to Lady Blanch? Is Violet in danger?

Cierra shook her head, pushing aside the troubling thoughts. Dwelling on them wouldn't achieve anything. Retreating to her room, with heavy eyelids and a weary heart, she changed into her pyjamas, got into bed, and surrendered to the embrace of exhaustion.

Hours passed in a blur of restless dreams, until finally, Cierra noticed the harsh light of day seeping in through the gap in her curtains. Blinking away the remnants of sleep, she lay in bed for a while, grappling with the weight of the revelation she had discovered in the night.

She wanted answers, but a part of her was afraid to find out what Violet had been hiding.

Cierra took her time getting out of bed and getting dressed, gathering her thoughts and steeling herself for the conversation that needed to happen. Only when she felt confident in her ability to maintain her composure did she emerge from her room to speak to Violet, who was now back from the market and sitting on the sofa in the lounge area.

"Are you in debt to Lady Blanch?" Cierra asked, wasting no time in getting to the point.

"The landlady?" Violet asked, an anxious squeak in her voice.

Every time Violet has mentioned the landlady of this building, she has been referring to Lady Blanch?! I had no idea!

"Yes," Cierra confirmed matter-of-factly. "The landlady."

"A few years ago, I fell on hard times," Violet said hesitantly. "I couldn't afford to pay the rent, so Lady Blanch told me I could pay it at a later date. Admittedly, she has added a fair bit of interest over the years. I'll pay it back eventually."

"I see," said Cierra.

"Anyway," said Violet, her tone now defensive, "why are you asking?"

As Cierra slumped onto the familiar comfort of the sofa, a heavy sigh escaped her lips. She then buried her face in her hands. She couldn't fault Violet for the choices she had made, but it pained her to know that her friend probably didn't know about mutants, and that her debt was therefore a looming danger.

"I wish you could have told me before," Cierra said as she lifted her face from her palms to look at Violet. "You know I would have chipped in to help. You know I wouldn't have sat back and let you struggle. I could have..."

"No, you couldn't," Violet said softly. "You protect people, Cierra. I know that much about what you do, and I understand that your income isn't regular. If my part in making this town a better place is to give you food and a home without you having to worry about rent, then so be it."

"You don't understand," Cierra said, touched by Violet's thoughtful nature, but worried about her naivety.

"How can I?" said Violet, dismayed. "I know nothing of the world you live in. It's not your fault. I know there are things you can't tell me for my own safety. But just as much as I'm not in your world, you're not in mine."

Cierra had always assumed that Violet would confide in her if she needed help. Although they respected each other's privacy, they had always had each other's backs. Nevertheless, it was clear to Cierra that Violet hadn't sought to deceive her. She could feel it in every fibre of her being.

"All I can tell you right now is that Lady Blanch is a terrible, evil woman who can't be trusted," Cierra finally said. "Please, Violet, don't give her any reason to turn her focus onto you."

Chapter Six

Sitting in the quiet solitude of her bedroom, already dressed for action, impatience gnawed at Cierra as she eagerly kept her eye on the time. Not only was she keen to meet up with Taryn for the good of the town, but now that she knew Violet was in debt to Lady Blanch, the mission was personal.

Just minutes before sunset, Cierra climbed out of the third-floor window. Enjoying the sensation of the crisp air of the outdoors against her skin, she gracefully began to make her way across the rooftops. Navigating swiftly, she reached the designated meeting spot ahead of time, her eyes darting around sharply in anticipation of Taryn's arrival.

As the minutes stretched beyond twilight, Taryn remained conspicuously absent, causing alarm bells to ring in Cierra's mind. Assassins were never late for a rendezvous unless something bad had prevented them from getting there on time. In a heightened state of alertness, Cierra waited and waited, but still Taryn didn't appear.

Cierra hesitated, torn between the idea of pursuing Taryn and the fear of missing each other in a futile chase. Time was slipping away, urging her to make a decision. She couldn't linger here, not if something had gone wrong.

In a swift motion, she retrieved a handkerchief and a marker pen from one of her pockets. Resting the handkerchief on her knee and folding it meticulously, she inscribed a bold letter 'C' on its surface. She then tucked it under a loose tile, ensuring that it was positioned discreetly, but would be noticeable to Taryn in the event of her arrival.

Satisfied that the marked handkerchief would succinctly convey to Taryn that she had been waiting for her, Cierra left the meeting point, leaping with determination across rooftops in search of any clue that could lead her to Taryn's whereabouts.

Cierra's challenge lay in not knowing where Taryn lived, or of the other areas that she frequented. The mystery shrouding the other assassin's movements made tracking her down seem like an insurmountable task. Nevertheless, Cierra persisted, scouring the vicinity and expanding outwards into the darkness.

Her quest led her to leap onto a rooftop where an unsettling sensation greeted her; her hand brushed against something sticky on a ledge. Raising her hand to inspect it, the metallic scent of blood immediately assaulted her senses.

A wave of dread washed over her as she looked up from her hand and focused on the tiles up ahead. There was a trail of fresh blood. She reasoned that the blood could only be Taryn's, for nobody else was in the habit of frequenting the town's rooftops.

Cierra followed the trail of blood, which led her to climb down from the roof via a drainpipe. Turning her attention to the cobblestones in front of her, she quickly noticed that the trail continued across the road before abruptly ending. It indicated that whoever was responsible for Taryn's injuries must have swiftly transported her away – there was no way her bleeding would have ceased so suddenly on its own.

The silence that hung over the deserted road only added to the eerie atmosphere. Whatever secrets this desolate trail held, Cierra knew she needed to find out more, and that time could be of the essence.

Following the path a carriage must have taken, Cierra suddenly caught a pungent scent of blood so overwhelming that instinctively, she sensed it was from multiple sources.

As she gazed at a looming disused warehouse ahead, a realisation struck her like a bolt of lightning. This had to be a mutant den, a place she had only heard of in training, and even then it had been the stuff of legend. Cierra had been told that mutant dens were dark, foreboding places where twisted creatures gathered to feast on the blood of captive humans.

Clenching her jaw, she knew she needed to tread carefully. She couldn't just barge in and try to take them all on at once, for one wrong move could lead to her demise in such hostile territory. She needed a strategy.

She circled to the rear of the building, hoping to find windows for a glimpse inside. Unfortunately though, they had all been covered with boards, leaving only narrow openings. Through one of them, she could barely see figures moving within.

Just as she was trying to get a better look, her heart leapt into her throat when she heard a piercing female scream.

Taryn?!

Abandoning caution, Cierra's adrenaline surged as she ripped one of the boards off a broken window. Hoisting herself up, she twisted her body through the tight opening, feeling splinters of glass catching against her leather bodysuit as she pushed forward.

As her feet softly touched down upon the neglected flooring of the building, she found herself in the midst of chaos, facing a crowd of mutants. Some bore almost humanlike features, whilst others were hunched over with gnarled, misshapen bodies, resembling something out of a nightmare. All of them had their gaze fixed on her.

Quickly scanning the area beyond what was immediately in front of her, Cierra caught sight of Taryn, who was restrained in a chair at the opposite end of the large room. There was a gash on her leg where part of her bodysuit had been torn away. Blood seeped from the wound, gathering in a small pool on the floor that two particularly eager mutants were greedily licking up.

Reacting swiftly, Cierra unsheathed her twin blades. Glowing an urgent hue of magenta, they were ready for use. The very sight caused the mutants around her to take a step back, exchanging wary glances amongst themselves as though they were carefully considering their next move.

Suddenly, the mutants began to act with focus. Like a raging tide, their movements were no longer those of individual beings, but rather a collective force, treading menacingly towards Cierra. Each step was a display of power and determination, their eyes wild with fury as they progressed towards their target.

The sound of their feet stomping against the wooden floorboards echoed in Cierra's ears, drowning out all other noises except for the occasional grunt or cry. It was like being caught in the midst of a storm.

Cierra's muscles tensed as she braced herself for the onslaught. As the first mutant lunged at her with a feral snarl, she met it with a swift and precise strike from one of her blades. The mutant howled in pain as the blade tore through its flesh, but that didn't stop it from charging forward again.

Cierra fiercely spun out of the way and delivered another blow to the mutant's neck, decapitating it. She then turned her attention to those who were closing in on her.

Taking on one after another, she slashed and stabbed with expert precision, honed from years of training. Her blades glowed brighter with each strike, slicing through flesh and bone like butter. Blood sprayed and splattered around her, mixing with the stench of rotting flesh and sweat in a nauseating cocktail.

Without faltering, Cierra kept moving, using both blades to keep the mutants at bay. Some tried to grab onto her with their gnarled hands, but she evaded them with ease. Others attempted to use makeshift weapons against her – chair legs and shards of broken glass, no doubt left over from when the warehouse had seen better days – but they were no match for her agility and skill.

As the last remaining mutants retreated, Cierra took a moment to catch her breath. She quickly scanned the room, making sure there were no more immediate threats lurking in the shadows. The few mutants that remained stood around fearfully, hesitant to take their chances against Cierra and her blades.

Satisfied that it was now safe enough, Cierra made her way towards Taryn, who looked pale with beads of sweat dripping down her brow.

"I'm grateful," said Taryn, exhaustion in her voice, "but you took one hell of a risk coming here to save me."

Working quickly to free Taryn from her bonds, Cierra said nothing. Her entire focus was set on untying the coarse ropes.

"Let's get out of here," she said to Taryn as she cut through the last of the knots with a pocket knife.

With bated breath, Cierra waited for Taryn to move. As Taryn rose from her seat, it was clear that something was wrong. Her movements were slow and unsteady, her steps laboured as though she was fighting through intense pain. As she struggled to put weight on her injured leg, Cierra couldn't help but wince.

"Go ahead without me," Taryn said, sincerity in her eyes.

"No way," Cierra insisted.

Deciding that they would need to escape without being followed by the remaining mutants who were still milling around, Cierra delved into one of her pockets to retrieve a smoke bomb. Hurling the ball of powder at the floor with certainty, she held her breath as thick, grey smoke billowed into the air, obscuring their surroundings.

Hearing the sound of mutants coughing and spluttering amidst the grit and ash, Cierra swiftly concealed her blades, and then scooped Taryn up into her arms. Holding her tightly, she headed for the nearest exit.

Chapter Seven

Stepping out into the street, Cierra deeply inhaled the fresh air of the night, relieved to be free of the smoke inside the building.

As she began to walk with Taryn still in her arms, she faltered a little beneath the weight.

"I told you to leave me behind," Taryn said grumpily, despite how the ghost of a grateful smile played on her lips.

Knowing that Taryn's injured leg would make it impossible for them to get up onto the rooftops together, Cierra was determined to make her way through the streets.

"We've come this far," she told Taryn. "Now isn't the time to give up."

"Seriously, Cierra," said Taryn. "It's great that you've got me out of there, but we both know that if you insist on carrying me, it will only slow you down."

Taryn was right. In a matter of time, if the mutants in the warehouse wanted to, they could easily barge out onto the street, rejuvenated and prepared to attack.

"I'm not leaving you," Cierra said defiantly. "Besides, I'm sure there will come a point where I'll need you to help me. I have never seen a mutant den before; whatever the nature of this plague of enemies on the town, I don't fancy taking it on alone."

Deciding that another smoke bomb would buy them some time by obscuring the view of any emerging mutants, Cierra reached into one of her pockets. The moment she hurled the offending item at the ground, thick plumes of heavy smoke began to billow around them.

Leaving the spreading smoke behind, with Taryn still securely in her arms, Cierra moved along the streets as quickly as she could, her muscles burning as she scanned the area in search of a place to hide.

Finally, she spotted an alleyway tucked between two buildings. She hurried into it.

After doing a quick check of the area to be certain that the coast was clear, Cierra gently eased Taryn down onto the ground. As soon as Taryn's back made contact with the cobblestones, it became clear to Cierra that her fellow assassin's condition had deteriorated. Taryn was mumbling incoherently. Through her slurred speech, she seemed confused.

"My…" she uttered, her eyes rolling back a little. "I think I…"

"It's ok," Cierra reassured, not quite convinced of her own words. "Just relax. I'm going to help you."

Looking down at Taryn's leg, Cierra noticed that blood was still seeping from the deep gash on the side of her calf. Reacting quickly, Cierra reached into a pocket and pulled out several white handkerchiefs. She deftly wrapped the fabric around Taryn's lower leg, creating a makeshift bandage to cover the wound. Her nimble fingers expertly tied the handkerchief corners together, securing the fabric in place. She knew that stopping Taryn's bleeding was not only important in and of itself, but also to prevent a trail of blood, which would surely attract more mutants.

With Taryn in such a state, Cierra reasoned that their best option would be to seek refuge back home. In terms of the need to keep things secret from Violet, it wouldn't be ideal, but it was the nearest point of safety in the circumstances.

"Come on," said Cierra, using every ounce of strength to pull Taryn upright so she could lift her again.

Chapter Eight

As Cierra approached her building, the weight of Taryn's limp body in her arms felt like an anchor dragging her down. Every step seemed like an effort, but finally, she reached the familiar entrance, relief flooding through her like a rushing tide.

Once inside, navigating the narrow stairwell proved treacherous, the darkness seeming to conspire against Cierra with every step.

"Hold on," she muttered to Taryn, her arms trembling with exertion as they ascended.

Fuelled by determination, Cierra pressed on, her muscles straining with the effort as she climbed up to the third floor.

At last, the door to home loomed before them like a beacon of safety. With a burst of adrenaline-fuelled strength, Cierra leaned into it to push it open, practically stumbling into the living room with Taryn's unconscious form slumping heavily against her.

Violet's shocked gasp echoed through the room as she took in the scene before her.

"What's going on?!" she exclaimed, her eyes wide with concern.

"Get the medical kit," Cierra commanded, her voice sharp with urgency. "It's under my bed. Hurry!"

As Violet darted away to fetch the medical kit, Cierra diligently lowered Taryn to the floor, her movements swift and sure despite the uncertainty of the situation.

With cautious hands, Cierra gingerly peeled away the makeshift bandage from Taryn's leg. In her fear of aggravating the wound further, each movement was deliberate. As the fabric came away, revealing the raw, still-bleeding gash beneath, Cierra's breath caught in her throat, her mind racing as she assessed the situation.

That wound has been bleeding for a while now. I wonder if the mutants used an anticoagulant.

"We need towels," she called out to Violet, her voice tight with tension. "And water – warm, if you can."

As the dissonance in the room hung heavy, Violet returned with a bundle of supplies clutched tightly in her arms – towels, a bowl of warm water, and the medical kit. With a determined expression, she approached Cierra, her demeanour full of empathy.

"Here," she said softly, placing everything down next to Cierra. "Whatever you need, I'm here to help."

"Thanks," Cierra said gratefully, already placing the towels beneath Taryn's leg.

"Is she going to be ok?" Violet asked after a long pause, her voice tinged with fear.

"I don't know," Cierra admitted as she applied pressure to the wound, "but we have to try."

Suddenly, Taryn stirred, her voice barely

above a whisper as she struggled to make sense of her surroundings.

"Where... am I?" she murmured, her eyes fluttering open.

"You're safe," Cierra reassured, her voice soft yet firm. "Just keep calm, and stay still, ok?"

Taryn grunted and closed her eyes.

"I'm sorry for barging in on you like this," Cierra said, her words laden with sincerity as she turned to address Violet.

"Is this the person who gave you that letter?" Violet asked.

"Yes," said Cierra. "Her name's Taryn."

Inspecting the wound more closely, Cierra noticed how jagged and raw it looked. Her hands trembled slightly as she debated whether or not it would need stitching. First though, as a matter of priority, she took out a glass jar of paste from the medical kit. Scooping out a liberal amount of the charcoal-scented sage-coloured concoction, she spread a thick layer of it over the wound.

Then, deciding to use stitches only as a last resort to allow for further monitoring, she set about applying a fresh bandage – this time a large piece of fabric rather than a makeshift assortment of handkerchiefs.

"Sorry," Cierra said softly, noticing how the sensation of the paste settling in was causing Taryn to wince in discomfort.

"Solstice," Taryn said with certainty, shakily sitting up a little to grip Cierra's arm. "They're planning... Solstice."

"Solstice. Got it," Cierra acknowledged, simply humouring Taryn so that she could rest and recover.

"*Solstice*," Taryn uttered again, the urgency in her voice coming through despite her weakened state.

"You need to rest, Taryn," Cierra said soothingly. "You're going to be ok, but you need to rest."

Taryn had no choice but to comply. Groaning in frustration, she settled back down on the floor and closed her eyes, seeming appreciative that she was now safe. The stillness of the room only highlighted the sound of her slow, steady breathing as she drifted off into a deep sleep.

"Please tell me what's going on," Violet said gently, kneeling down next to Cierra and placing a hand on her shoulder. "Please, tell me everything. I can't be left in the dark anymore."

In view of everything that had happened, Cierra couldn't deny that Violet's request was entirely reasonable. And so, whilst keeping a vigilant watch over Taryn, she took a seat on the sofa next to Violet. Starting at the beginning, she then told her friend everything.

Chapter Nine

Several hours had passed, with nighttime easing into daylight. During that time, apart from when Cierra had stitched the wound on Taryn's leg, the injured assassin had slept soundly. Although Cierra was exhausted, she was relieved to know that Taryn was over the worst of her injury and was going to be ok. She was no longer bleeding. If indeed the mutants had used an anticoagulant, the paste had served to remedy the effects.

Although Cierra's revelations had come as a shock to Violet at first, it hadn't taken long for Violet to become accepting of the situation, having always known that Cierra only wanted to help the town and its people. On board with everything that Cierra had revealed, Violet promised to stay home all day, insisting that she would watch over

Taryn while Cierra got some much-needed rest.

As she lay in her bed, Cierra drifted in and out of a fitful sleep, anxious to make sense of what Taryn had been trying to tell her.

Solstice? Why did she keep saying 'solstice'? And so urgently too! What could it mean? Tomorrow is the solstice, but Taryn made it sound more important than that.

Deciding that Taryn had perhaps been trying to communicate something that was time-sensitive, and satisfied that her fellow assassin would be ok with Violet, Cierra didn't want to wait around. With everything that had been going on, she didn't want to risk leaving anything to chance.

Her jaw set with determination, Cierra left her bed and marched towards her bedroom window, her shoulders squared and her gaze focused ahead. Opening the window and jumping out onto a neighbouring roof with ease, she squinted against the sunlight.

She moved quickly and stealthily across the rooftops, keeping to the shadows and avoiding any potential observers down on the cobblestones below. She had always been more accustomed to travelling at night, but she couldn't afford to wait until then to make her way towards Lady Blanch's manor.

Approaching the rooftop opposite the manor, Cierra slowed down and surveyed the area. The large, sprawling estate was surrounded by a tall stone wall, with the main entrance guarded by two muscular-looking men, each armed with a bow and arrow. Cierra could also see several guards stationed around the perimeter of the grounds, making it clear that Lady Blanch took her security seriously.

Cierra knew that trying to sneak into the manor in broad daylight would be foolish. She figured that whilst waiting for darkness to arrive, she would use the time to plan her entry strategy.

From her vantage point, she keenly scanned every detail of the imposing manor before her. With a calculated gaze, she made note of all potential entrance points. Moving along the rows of tiles beneath her, she soon realised that there were more windows than guards, who were all staunchly focused on just the doors.

There's no room for error, but if I can quickly enter through the right window at the right time, I'll have to face whatever happens once I'm inside.

After one final observation of the surroundings, Cierra decided that instead of waiting for hours, she would use the time to go back home and check on Taryn.

***

Stepping through the window into her bedroom, Cierra noticed immediately that it was eerily quiet.

"Hello?" she called out. "Taryn? Violet?"

There was no reply.

Cierra fruitlessly searched every room, her heart pounding with worry. Frustrated, she began to pace around the living area.

Where are they?! Taryn should still be resting, and Violet should be here too.

Immediately, Cierra could hear the sound of heavy footsteps echoing from down the hallway. As they slowly thudded along, they sounded nothing like Violet's or Taryn's.

Cierra's muscles tensed, her fingers clenching tightly around the hilt of one of her concealed blades. A feeling of unease settled over her like a heavy cloak as she sensed danger lurking.

Suddenly, Lady Blanch appeared, emerging menacingly from the darkness, causing tendrils of fear to coil around Cierra's heart. As the tall woman's towering figure loomed, it cast a shadow that seemed to stretch on endlessly. Cierra couldn't help but feel dwarfed by the sheer presence of the imposing figure just a couple of metres away from her.

Lady Blanch's smile sent a chill down Cierra's spine. It was not the warm, inviting smile of a friend or ally, but rather a twisted, maniacal grin that seemed to stretch unnaturally across the mutant woman's face. The corners of her lips curled upwards in a grotesque parody of mirth, revealing teeth stained beige with tobacco, and crimson with blood.

In an effort to divert her gaze, Cierra noticed

that the woman's skin was unnaturally pale and smeared with a thick layer of white makeup, hiding any imperfections. Clutching a gnarled cane in her right hand, the abnormally tall woman tapped its twisted form against the floor, authority in her every movement. Even indoors, she wore a wide-brimmed hat, the same dark grey colour as her long gown of flowing chiffon – its delicate fabric hugging her gaunt-but-womanly figure. Resting on her exposed chest was a pendant holding a red jewel, ancient and priceless. Overall, the woman's elegant façade contrasted with her identity as a powerful mutant.

"Oh, Cierra," Lady Blanch said, her voice sweet and condescending. "I didn't expect to see you here. After all, you're not on the lease."

Cierra winced. The woman was right.

"I'm a friend of Violet's," Cierra retorted, determined not to be intimidated. "Can I help you?"

"As a matter of fact, you can," said Lady Blanch, walking calmly across the room to put a hand on the sofa, effortlessly taking command of the space, "by staying out of my business."

Cierra blinked. It certainly wasn't the response she'd been expecting.

"We had such a great arrangement, you and I," the mutant woman said. "I left you alone to do whatever you wanted, and you kept out of my way."

"Excuse me?"

"I know who you are," Lady Blanch clarified. "I know *what* you are. I've turned a blind eye to your presence, but if you persist in poking your nose where it doesn't belong, we're going to have problems."

Cierra couldn't allow herself to be overpowered.

"Where's Taryn? Where's Violet?" she demanded.

"As I said," Lady Blanch answered, taking a broad and intimidating step towards Cierra, "it's not possible for me to ignore your presence when you seem so enthused about mine. I've made sure to take care of Taryn and Violet – just as a little insurance policy, I'm sure you'll understand."

"What?! Where are they? What have you..."

"Oh, don't worry," Lady Blanch interrupted, delighting in Cierra's distress. "They're alive and well enough – for now, at least. I just thought it would be fair to let you know that if you insist on getting in my business, the situation is subject to change."

Despite the flurry of words that raced through Cierra's mind, none of them left her mouth. She was too shocked, too angry.

"I'm glad we had this little chat, Cierra. Now that we understand each other, I trust that I won't be seeing you again."

With an air of silent dominance, Lady Blanch turned away from Cierra, her movements graceful, yet laden with an unspoken threat. Her demeanour spoke volumes, leaving Cierra paralysed with a sense of foreboding. As the mutant woman calmly let herself out of the front door, the atmosphere in the room seemed to constrict, suffocating Cierra with its oppressive weight.

Chapter Ten

Standing alone in the lounge area, fuelled with blind rage, seething with fury, Cierra clenched her fists. Although Lady Blanch had left a good few minutes ago, the weight of her menacing words still hung in the air.

"How dare she?!" Cierra uttered under her breath, her voice reverberating with righteous indignation, each word dripping with venom.

I need to get my head together. I can't afford to give in to my emotions right now.

In her conscious effort to approach the situation rationally, Cierra's mind finally began to clear. Despite the tremor of fear that lingered beneath the surface, she knew that Taryn and Violet's fate lay in her hands, their lives hanging in the balance with each passing second.

Although she knew that Taryn possessed a great level of skill, Cierra couldn't shake the nagging worry that her fellow assassin could still be weak from her run-in with the mutants in the warehouse. As for Violet, Cierra was certain that her friend's gentle nature and livelihood as a flower seller would render her ill-equipped to face the likes of Lady Blanch.

Just thinking back to the blood stains that marred Lady Blanch's malicious smile served to remind Cierra that the mutant could easily decide to drink from her friends, bleeding them dry. After all, what good would it do the evil woman to release her captives now?

There's only one thing for it. Not only do I need to rescue Taryn and Violet, but I need to take out Lady Blanch. It's time to put an end to her reign of terror.

Knowing that she couldn't strike until darkness, Cierra decided that she would need to be in top form when the time arrived.

Determined and resolute, for the benefit of her mind as well as her body, she strode over to the kitchen area. First, she reached for a tender cut of lean beef, marbled with just the right amount of fat to impart flavour and energy. Next, she selected a handful of fresh vegetables, vibrant and colourful, each one bursting with vitamins and minerals essential for maintaining her stamina.

Slicing and dicing, she threw everything together in the pan. As the ingredients sizzled and mingled together, her anticipation grew. Knowing that each bite would fuel her body for the challenges that lay ahead, with a sense of purpose driving her movements, she stirred, ensuring that every last morsel would cook to perfection.

Feeling pleased with herself that she had managed to stay in control of her mind and do something constructive in the wait for sundown, after plating up the meal, Cierra sat down to eat. She savoured every bite as it filled her with strength and resolve – she would need it in order to have a fighting chance against such a formidable adversary.

***

No thanks to the impending solstice, night had finally fallen over the town of Willowbrook. Cierra, her belly full from earlier, was crouched down on the edge of a rooftop, relying on the light of the gas lamps below to assist in her surveillance of the area.

Satisfied that it was now time to move, she began to travel across the rooftops, her figure a silent shadow against the moonlit sky. Below, the steady clip-clop of horse-drawn carts echoed through the night, mingling with the occasional murmur of conversation from people passing by, no doubt on their way home from the taverns after having stayed out a little longer, what with it being so close to the longest day of the year.

Unfazed by the presence of others due to her ability to remain unseen, with each leap and bound, Cierra navigated the rooftops with the grace of a skilled acrobat, her movements fluid and precise.

As she approached Lady Blanch's imposing manor, her heart quickened with anticipation. Despite this, she remained focused and calculated with every step.

Touching down on the familiar roof opposite the manor, Cierra crouched low, her bleach-white hair blending seamlessly with the silver moonlight as she took a moment to survey her surroundings.

Her eyes narrowed as she observed the guards patrolling the perimeter, each of them alert and armed.

Just as I expected.

Cierra had been right in her assumptions earlier that day: she would have to enter the manor via a window. The challenge now was in deciding which one would be the best option, for there was no shortage of choice. It frustrated her that whichever window she chose, she had no control over what she could be walking into. If she was lucky, she could find Taryn and Violet straight away. Considering the size of the building though, the odds were not in her favour.

Deciding to search for a point of entry that would grant her access to the manor whilst minimising her chances of being spotted by the guards below, Cierra's gaze eventually settled upon a fourth-floor window. It appeared to be partially open.

That's the one, she told herself, her resolve hardening. *Time to make my move.*

With certainty, Cierra launched herself from the roof, her body cutting through the night air like a silent arrow. As she neared the target window, she channelled all of her skills, all of her stamina.

Reaching out a gloved hand to grasp the ivy-covered ledge, she prayed that luck would be on her side as she prepared to infiltrate Lady Blanch's home.

Chapter Eleven

With her pulse throbbing in her ears, Cierra gracefully swung her legs over the ledge and carefully slid through the narrow opening of the window. Her muscles tensed as she maintained a tight grip on the frame, her fingers digging into the hard wood.

Deftly landing on the polished marble floor inside the large house, the soles of her boots made no sound.

Of all the rooms to end up in... she thought, her eyes adjusting to the dim light as she took in the opulence surrounding her.

The large private bathroom spoke volumes of Lady Blanch's wealth and vanity. The floor and walls were covered in pristine white tiles, so bright that the gold taps of the sink and bath could be seen in them. The bathtub itself, with claw-shaped feet, stood in the centre of the room, its porcelain surface gleaming beneath the low light of the moon outside.

As Cierra glanced around, her gaze fell upon several cupboards filled with an extravagant assortment of makeup. Foundations, powders, and lipsticks in various shades cluttered the shelves, indicating just how hard Lady Blanch had to work in her meticulous efforts to maintain her human façade.

Her curiosity piqued, Cierra couldn't resist taking a closer look at the collection of cosmetic products. She picked up a glass jar of thick foundation, noting the heavy consistency designed to cover Lady Blanch's unnatural pallor.

After silently putting the jar back in its place, Cierra carefully opened another cupboard. Nausea churned in her stomach at the sight before her: rows of sinister-looking instruments, their metallic surfaces polished to a shine. Empty tubes and vials filled the shelves – all designed for one sickening purpose: to aid Lady Blanch in her consumption of human blood.

As Cierra studied the paraphernalia, one particular detail caught her attention: the clean needles, neatly arranged. Her brow furrowed in confusion and disgust. Why would someone like Lady Blanch need these? It seemed unlikely that she'd bother with the pretence of cleanliness when taking blood by force.

Unless... Cierra considered, the horrifying truth dawning on her, *she's not just hunting her victims down, killing them and bleeding them dry. She's repeatedly getting some of her blood from the same people as a matter of routine – most likely by intimidation.*

Anger surged through Cierra as she considered the extent of Lady Blanch's disregard for everyone around her. She vowed that she couldn't let this continue.

Taking a deep breath to steel her resolve, Cierra quietly slipped out of the bathroom. As she crept down a dimly lit hallway, her movements silenced by the plush red carpet beneath her, she couldn't help but imagine the horrors that Lady Blanch perhaps had in store for Violet and Taryn.

Cautiously moving further down the hallway, Cierra kept close to the wall. Her mind raced with plans and contingencies, trying to anticipate any obstacles that might stand between her and her friends.

Where would a twisted, bloodsucking mutant keep her captives? she wondered as she scanned the many doors lining the hallway.

She knew the chances of stumbling upon her friends before encountering Lady Blanch would be slim, but she held on to that hope like a lifeline. The sheer size of the manor made her feel as though she was a single drop of water in a vast ocean, yet she pressed forward with determination.

Relying on her instincts honed by years of experience as an assassin, she allowed herself to be drawn down the hallways, guided by her intuition and listening for any sign of Taryn and Violet. Her senses were on high alert, hyperaware of her surroundings.

As she rounded a corner, she caught a

glimpse of a grand staircase spiralling upwards. She hesitated for a moment, wondering if she should ascend the stairs or continue along the hallway. However, her thoughts were interrupted by the sound of approaching footsteps, thudding and heavy.

Cierra darted into the nearest room, praying that she wouldn't be seen. She pressed her back against the wall, its thick paper textured and soft. Her breath was shallow and rapid, her body coiled like a spring, prepared to strike at the first sign of danger.

Growing louder, the footsteps drew closer. Cierra held her breath, her heart hammering in her chest as she braced herself in preparation to strike. Luckily though, the footsteps continued past the doorway, gradually fading into the distance.

That was too close!

Satisfied that whoever it was had disappeared around a corner, Cierra took the opportunity to get her bearings.

Shrouded in darkness, the room was chaotic. Cierra's eyes darted around, taking note of the disarray. An exceptionally large bed lay unmade, its sheets tangled and strewn across the mattress. Untidily arranged, pots of makeup, tubes of lipstick, and hairpins littered the surfaces of several dressing tables. Every mirror on each of the several dressing tables was shattered, the irregular shards of glass displaying a disorientating reflection.

What a mess!

Suddenly, a faint creaking sound broke the silence. Convinced that it had come from the doorway behind her, Cierra was hit by a sickening sinking feeling. She could sense a presence, unseen, but unmistakable. Every nerve in her body screamed with alarm, and she registered, without a doubt, that she was not alone.

Chapter Twelve

"Did you think you could just waltz into my home without consequences, dear?"

Cierra's blood ran cold as she instantly recognised the voice. With a hand on one of her blades in its sheath, she whipped around to face Lady Blanch.

"Surprised to see me?" the mutant woman asked, a sinister smile playing on her lips.

Her tall, elegant frame towered over Cierra, the length of her grey chiffon dress rustling softly as she stepped closer.

"Such nerve you have, trespassing in my domain," Lady Blanch said with a sneer, her slender fingers gripping the handle of her pipe as she brought it to her lips.

The scent of tobacco filled the room as the mutant woman exhaled, slowly and deliberately towards Cierra. Disgusted by the intimidation tactics, Cierra cringed as the smoke billowed around her, assaulting her senses.

"Back off," Cierra retorted firmly.

Although attempting to kill Lady Blanch would be dangerous, Cierra knew that within the confines of the cluttered bedroom with no one else around, this could be her best chance.

"What a pity that you couldn't just keep out of my business," Lady Blanch said with malice as she set her pipe aside. "Let's see what you're truly made of."

The moment the mutant woman began walking towards her, each footstep menacing and deliberate, Cierra's instincts kicked in, causing her to draw her blades.

Unafraid to fight dirty, Lady Blanch surveyed her surroundings with a predatory gaze. Spotting a metal candlestick holder on the nearest dressing table, she wasted no time in grabbing hold of it, her fingers curling around the weighty piece with fierce conviction.

With a swift, fluid motion, the mutant woman hurled the makeshift weapon at Cierra, sending it flying through the air with deadly intent.

Reflexively, Cierra managed to dodge the incoming projectile. It sailed past her in a blur, and then, with a resounding crash, it smashed through the bedroom window, sending shards of glass flying outward into the night.

As the echoes of the impact reverberated through the room, Cierra, sharp and alert, observed the anger on her opponent's face. This was far from over.

"Insufferable wretch," Lady Blanch said with a snarl.

Driven by a combination of hatred and blind rage, the obscenely tall woman charged at Cierra, swiping through the air with her large hands. Cierra rolled to the side, narrowly avoiding the mutant's grasp. Her heart raced as she realised just how strong and determined her opponent was.

Cierra lunged forward, swift and precise as she aimed to strike Lady Blanch with lethal precision. To her dismay though, Lady Blanch was proving to be faster and more agile than she had been anticipating.

Lady Blanch, with a fluid grace that belied her towering stature, deftly avoided Cierra's blades, her every movement a calculated evasion. Each strike was avoided with a quick sidestep, leaving the mutant woman unscathed and poised to retaliate.

Cierra's surprise quickly turned to frustration as her blows failed to find their mark, her blades slicing through empty air with each missed opportunity. It was clear that Lady Blanch was a formidable adversary.

"Is that all you've got?" Lady Blanch taunted, her voice dripping with contempt. "You cannot hope to win against me."

With her unnaturally tall frame looming ominously, Lady Blanch's menacing smile stretched across her face like a grotesque mask. With a chilling determination in her eyes, she lunged at Cierra, her movements fast and predatory. As she closed the distance between them, the sheer force of her approach carried a warning of impending doom, her towering presence growing more intimidating, her shadow casting a pall over the room like a harbinger of darkness.

Her eyes gleaming with insatiable hunger, the mutant woman leaned in towards Cierra, her mouth wide and her teeth pointed at the assassin's neck. With a guttural growl, she prepared to sink her teeth into Cierra's flesh.

In a flash of terror, Cierra had no doubt that her opponent was entirely capable and willing to drink her blood, and would delight in watching her die a slow, agonising death.

With a fierce battle cry, her blades flashing a furious shade of magenta, Cierra fought tooth and nail to fend off her monstrous adversary. In that moment, it was clear that only one of them would emerge victorious from this deadly confrontation, and Cierra was determined to ensure that it would be her.

Knowing that she needed to take the upper hand, and fast, with a surge of adrenaline, Cierra quickly ducked down, dropped one of her blades, and grabbed at Lady Blanch, succeeding to sweep the woman's legs out from under her. As the towering mutant crashed to the floor, Cierra swiftly retrieved her blade. Now armed with them both, she stood tall over Lady Blanch, pinning the woman down with a foot on her chest, and the sharp tip of a blade pointed with threatening certainty at her neck. The once-menacing smile disappeared from Lady Blanch's face to be replaced by a look of sheer terror.

"Please," she begged, gasping between heavy breaths, "please, don't kill me."

Cierra hesitated, her grip tightening on her blades. She could see the fear in Lady Blanch's eyes, and it stirred something within her. It was an unexpected moment of vulnerability from the woman.

"Give me one good reason why I shouldn't," Cierra said in a low voice, her tone cold and unwavering.

"Because... because I never asked for any of this," Lady Blanch choked out, desperate to avoid the tip of the blade pointing at her neck. "I hate myself. I hate what I've become, what I am. I'm a monster!"

"You are," Cierra said bluntly. "So why should I spare your life?"

"Look around you," Lady Blanch implored. "All the mirrors are broken – I can't stand to look at myself! I never wanted this; I never chose to be a mutant!"

"Then how did it happen?" Cierra asked, curiosity getting the better of her.

"When I was a child, a mere human child, I caught a terrible disease. The only way to save my life was through a blood transfusion. But the blood they gave me... it came from a human-presenting mutant. My parents, the doctor, none of them knew until it was too late. It cursed me with an insatiable hunger for blood. Every day since then, I've had to struggle with the monster inside me, fighting to keep it at bay, but to no avail."

Cierra's grip on her blades wavered as she

considered Lady Blanch's words. She had never imagined that there could be such pain and turmoil hidden beneath that cold, monstrous exterior. The weight of the decision before her felt crushing, and for a moment, she questioned whether killing Lady Blanch would truly be the right thing to do.

"Please," Lady Blanch whispered, her voice quivering with fear and vulnerability, "don't let me die like this."

Cierra couldn't deny the humanity she saw in Lady Blanch's eyes, or ignore the distress behind her words. Just as she was beginning to entertain the possibility of mercy, however, something shifted in the mutant woman's gaze. The desperation turned to cunning, and Cierra, having seen every trick in the book during her time as an assassin, knew she had been played.

I can't afford to be swayed by her stories. I have to finish this.

Noticing the change in Cierra's demeanour, Lady Blanch's eyes widened in horror as she realised her time was up.

"It's over," Cierra confirmed darkly.

Keeping the one blade against Lady Blanch's neck to prevent her from trying to escape, with a swift and forceful motion, Cierra plunged the second blade into her heart. A guttural scream tore from the mutant woman's throat, her body arching in agony. Her shaking hands flailed frantically around the blade, unable to grip it in her desperation to pull it free, which only seemed to intensify the pain.

"Don't fight it," Cierra said, her voice devoid of emotion, harnessed through years of experience.

The mutant woman grimaced as her body spasmed, her once-elegant hands clawing at the air. For a moment, it seemed as if she would never stop fighting, that she would cling to life by sheer force of will. But then, finally, her movements slowed, her eyes becoming glassy as her final breaths heaved their way out of her.

As blood pooled out around the dead mutant's body in a gruesome halo, Cierra withdrew her blade and wiped it clean on a nearby curtain, knowing that there was still work to be done. Taryn and Violet were still prisoners in the building and it was up to her to rescue them from this nightmare.

Chapter Thirteen

Cierra sprinted down the opulent hallways of Lady Blanch's manor. She couldn't afford to slow down – not when Taryn and Violet were still in danger. As she moved, her twin blades glinted in the low lighting.

Where are they? she wondered frantically, her eyes quickly scanning every door she passed for any sign of her friends.

As she turned a corner, Cierra came face-to-face with a guard. His eyes widened at the sight of the bloodstained assassin, so before he could react, she lunged forward.

"Where are the prisoners?" she demanded, the tip of her blade pressed against his throat.

"Th-they're in the east wing," he stuttered, "locked in a room on the third floor."

"Thank you," Cierra said coldly, before driving her blade into his heart.

She couldn't afford to leave any loose ends. With renewed determination, she raced in the direction of the east wing, a combination of fear and urgency driving her on. As she rounded each corner, her senses on high alert for any sign of danger, the weight of responsibility pressed down upon her; if she couldn't find Taryn and Violet, it could still be over for them in the company of Lady Blanch's guards.

I'll kill any guard I encounter. It's the only way.

Reaching the third floor of the east wing, Cierra moved swiftly and silently, her footsteps muffled by the thick carpeting beneath her feet. With so many doors to choose from, she wanted to shout for Taryn and Violet, but knew that the risk was too high. The last thing she wanted was to draw the attention of more guards; she couldn't afford to be outnumbered by the enemy at this vital point.

Weighing her options carefully, Cierra decided to try every door in the vicinity. Approaching each one with a trembling hand, she tested every handle. With every attempt, she prayed for a miracle, for a sign that fate was on her side. Yet, time and time again, her hopes were dashed as the doors swung open to reveal empty rooms devoid of any sign of her friends.

Room after room, she searched, her frustration mounting with each fruitless endeavour. Most of the doors yielded easily to her touch, swinging open to reveal nothing but dust-covered furniture and trinkets forgotten despite their high value. It was as if the very walls themselves were conspiring against her, mocking her efforts with their unyielding silence.

Approaching yet another door, when Cierra gripped the handle, it resisted. At the unmistakable sensation of a locked door, she felt relieved to think that maybe, just maybe, this could be the room.

Without hesitation, she drew upon every ounce of strength within her, channelling it into a powerful kick aimed squarely at the door. The sheer force of the blow caused the wood to shatter, the sound echoing through the hallway like a thunderclap.

For a moment, there was nothing but a ringing in her ears and the sound of her own ragged breaths. Then, as the dust settled and the echoes faded, she was able to see inside the room.

"Cierra!" Violet whispered urgently, blinking in disbelief.

"I knew she would come," Taryn said weakly, her efforts at stoicism betraying the trauma she had undoubtedly suffered.

Huddled together in a corner, their feet tied and their hands bound behind their backs, the pair looked bruised and battered.

Pushing her way through the large gap in the door, Cierra took a quick moment to look around. The room was small and suffocating, with mould creeping up the damp wallpaper. A single barred window offered a narrow view of the moonlit night, allowing shadows to be cast on the dust-covered hardwood floor. It angered Cierra to think of how in the luxurious building, some of the rooms had seemingly been reserved for the purpose of holding Lady Blanch's victims against their will.

"Lady Blanch is dead," Cierra muttered bluntly, getting straight to the point. "I killed her."

"Good riddance," Taryn said, perking up a little at the news.

Violet exhaled a long breath, as though a tremendous weight had been lifted from her shoulders.

"We need to get out of here," Cierra insisted, refusing to let anyone take it easy as she crouched down and began untying the ropes that held Violet and Taryn captive. "We need to be mindful of the guards."

As soon as Taryn stood up, Cierra passed her a blade.

"Use this," she instructed. "If you encounter a guard, kill them. Show no mercy."

"Sure thing," Taryn confirmed, a flicker of

determination flashing across her features despite her exhaustion.

"Violet," said Cierra, refusing to sugar-coat anything. "Stay close to me. As soon as we step out of this room, grab something to use as a makeshift weapon. Choose something either very heavy, or very sharp. Hopefully, Taryn and I will be able to protect you, but I don't want you to walk these hallways unarmed, understood?"

Violet gulped nervously and then responded with a firm nod. Cierra knew that this was a lot for the humble florist to take on, but in the circumstances, there was no easy or subtle way to explain to Violet the potential dangers that lay ahead.

"Right," said Cierra, taking one last glance around the space that had kept Taryn and Violet captive. "Let's move."

Chapter Fourteen

As Cierra, Taryn and Violet cautiously made their way out of the east wing, the two assassins kept their senses sharp, scanning for signs of guards. When the trio reached the second-floor balcony overlooking the grand staircase without incident, Cierra knew their luck wouldn't last forever; she could see guards below, who would surely notice them soon enough.

Her instincts screaming at her to move, Cierra guided Taryn and Violet into a nearby room, eager to remain unnoticed by the enemy. She closed the door behind them with a soft click, sealing them inside what must have been another of Lady Blanch's dressing chambers.

The room was cavernous, its high ceilings adorned with elaborate patterns. A large wardrobe stood in the corner, its dark wooden doors thrown open to reveal a collection of elegant gowns. Each outfit was tailored for the now-dead mutant's unnaturally tall frame, the rich fabrics and intricate embellishments speaking of her twisted sense of glamour.

"With those guards lurking, there's no way we can leave via the ground floor," Cierra muttered to Taryn and Violet.

"I agree," said Taryn, gripping the hilt of her borrowed blade tightly in case of the need to strike an intruder at short notice.

"We'll have to climb out of the window and hope that nobody sees us," Cierra said firmly.

Violet's face paled at the comment, but she nodded, knowing there was no other way.

Seeing the fear in her friend's eyes, Cierra touched her arm reassuringly.

"Stay close to me, ok? We'll make it out of here. We have to."

"Alright," Violet whispered, a tremble in her voice.

As they approached the large window to peer out into the night, the darkness seemed to stretch on forever, like a void waiting to swallow them whole. Nevertheless, it satisfied Cierra to know that the street was deserted.

"Alright," she whispered, sheathing her blade and motioning for Taryn to pass her the other one so she could sheath that too. "I'll go first, then Taryn. Violet, you follow. We'll catch you."

"I still wish there was another way," Violet said, her eyes wide with fear. "I'm not... I've never done anything like this before."

"I know," Cierra whispered gently. "Don't panic. Once it's over, you'll never have to do anything like it again. I promise."

Violet hesitated, but finally gave a resolute nod.

Quietly opening the window and relieved that it didn't protest, Cierra climbed out and then carefully eased herself into a sitting position on the outside windowsill, gripping the edge tightly. Her body tensed as she lowered herself down a nearby drainpipe, her muscles straining with the effort.

As soon as her feet touched the cobblestoned ground, she looked up to see Taryn following suit. The fellow assassin moved with grace and skill, descending the side of the building with ease. Cierra couldn't help but admire her friend's agility and precision, qualities that had served them both well in their dangerous line of work.

When Taryn touched down on the street, she briefly exchanged a relieved glance with Cierra before they both turned their attention to helping Violet.

Reaching into one of her many pockets, Cierra produced a folded piece of fabric, its edges worn from years of use. Adorned with brown and beige floral patterns, the fabric held a special place in her assassin's arsenal. Whether used to tie herself to drainpipes for challenging heights, or as a makeshift shawl to help her blend in with a crowd, it had aided Cierra significantly on many demanding occasions. Tonight, it would be the lifeline Violet needed to escape the clutches of Lady Blanch's manor.

"Here," Cierra said quietly, handing one end of the fabric to Taryn. "Hold this tight. We're going to catch Violet when she jumps."

"Understood," Taryn replied, her voice steady despite the tension of the moment.

From the window above, Violet's strawberry-blonde hair whipped around her face. She then disappeared from view, leaving Cierra and Taryn to exchange a glance of shared anxiety.

"Ready?" Taryn whispered, her grip on the fabric tightening.

"Ready," Cierra confirmed, her heart thumping wildly in her chest.

Time seemed to slow as Violet reappeared at the window and carefully began to climb out onto the ledge, her body tense and trembling. The sight of her vulnerability tugged at something within Cierra, prompting fierce feelings of protectiveness. Then, Violet faithfully took a leap into the abyss.

She plummeted towards them, her body twisting and turning in the air like a leaf caught in a storm. The moment she hit the makeshift net, both Cierra and Taryn grunted with the effort, straining against the sudden force. But they held firm, and together, they guided Violet safely to the ground.

"Well done, everyone," Taryn said breathily as she released her grip on the fabric. "We did it."

"Are you ok, Violet?" Cierra asked, concern colouring her tone as she checked her friend for any signs of injury.

"I-I'm fine," Violet stammered in shock and disbelief. "I can't believe... Thank you."

"Thank us later," Cierra said, her expression hardening. "Right now, we need to get away from here."

Chapter Fifteen

Cierra hastily led Taryn and Violet into the dark embrace of a nearby alley, the shadows swallowing them whole.

"Listen," she said firmly. "It won't be long before the guards find Lady Blanch's body and come looking for us. We've got to stay ahead of them."

"Where should we go?" Violet asked, still trying to catch her breath.

"First, we need to get you back home, where it's safe," Cierra said. "Taryn and I can handle whatever comes next, but you... you don't belong in this world."

"Are you sure?" Violet asked, her tone brimming with hesitance. "I don't want to be a burden, but I also don't want to be alone."

"Trust me," Cierra said gently, giving Violet's hand a reassuring squeeze. "You'll be safer at home. We'll make sure of it."

"Wait," Taryn whispered urgently. "There's something else we need to consider."

"What is it?" Cierra asked, scanning the darkness for any signs of danger.

"Tomorrow is the solstice," Taryn said in a low voice, worry etched across her features. "When the mutants had me captive in their den, I overheard them talking about their plan. They're going to strike on the evening of the solstice. Lady Blanch had them prepped to enslave every human in Willowbrook. Of course, Lady Blanch is dead now, but I doubt that will stop the mutants. They want blood on-tap. Besides, the plan was always based on the mutants from the den having to head the ambush. Lady Blanch was just going to sit back while they did her dirty work."

"Why the solstice?" Violet asked.

"From what I could make of what the mutants were saying amongst themselves," said Taryn, "the reasoning behind the plan being set for the solstice is based on how so many humans will be out celebrating – unsuspecting, inebriated, and mostly defenceless."

"That's disgusting," Cierra whispered angrily. "We need to stop them."

"There's so many of them though," Taryn said doubtfully. "You saw what it was like when you came to rescue me."

"Yeah," said Cierra. "This time though, we will be ready for them. With the solstice being so near, I propose that we attack tonight."

"You're right," said Taryn. "I came here to help Willowbrook, and that's what I'm going to do."

"We'll take extra weaponry," Cierra said confidently. "If it comes down to it, we'll set the den on fire. Keeping the humans of this town safe is more important than a mere building."

"I agree," said Taryn. "I can't justify showing them even a shred of mercy."

"First though," Cierra said as she turned to address Violet, "we need to get you home, and quickly."

As they crept through the back alleys of the town, constantly on the lookout for danger, Cierra's mind raced with violent possibilities and tactical schemes, her senses sharpened by the gravity of their mission. She knew that the mutants would be relentless, but so would she and Taryn.

At last, they arrived at Violet's building. As they ascended the stairs to her third-floor home, the tension in the air was palpable.

As the three of them entered the cosy home, Cierra's gaze swept over the familiar interior, checking for any signs of intrusion. Satisfied and relieved that they had no unexpected visitors, she then led Taryn to her room and quickly pulled out the storage unit from under her bed.

"Take these," she said, passing a set of twin blades to Taryn.

"Thanks," said Taryn, taking her time to get used to the feel of the slightly unfamiliar weaponry, her practice movements soon becoming more fluid and precise.

"We'll need every advantage we can get," Cierra said, her voice tinged with urgency as she rummaged through her supplies.

Turning her attention to the bags of smoke bombs and boxes of matches she had stashed away, she quickly grabbed them and began handing some to Taryn, whilst ensuring to fill her own pockets too.

"I'm convinced we'll need these," she said.

With their preparations complete, Cierra and Taryn made one last sweep of Violet's home, ensuring that all windows were securely locked and that Violet would be safe in their absence. Only when they were satisfied that their friend was secure did they make their way to the door.

Before leaving, Cierra turned to Violet, her expression serious.

"Lock the door behind us," she instructed firmly. "And don't open it for anyone other than us. Understood?"

"I'll keep it locked," Violet promised, the tremble in her voice betraying her fear.

As she stepped out into the hall with Taryn, Cierra couldn't help but feel a sense of foreboding settling over her like a thick fog. There was no turning back now; the fate of Willowbrook was in their hands.

Chapter Sixteen

T heir pockets bulging with smoke bombs and matches, Cierra and Taryn moved swiftly along the rooftops of Willowbrook, cautious that there could now be guards from Lady Blanch's manor on the streets below.

When they reached the outside area of the abandoned warehouse, touching down on ground level, the two assassins exchanged a silent glance, their eyes reflecting the determination that burned within them. They knew their mission would not be easy, but they were prepared to face the danger that lay ahead.

With cautious steps, they entered the building and each drew their blades, their senses alert to every sound and movement around them. The floorboards creaked beneath their weight, protesting the intrusion.

I'm sure the mutants will come as soon as they sense us.

The air hung thick with a foul stench, making Cierra's every breath feel as though she was inhaling spoiled meat.

Just as their eyes had adjusted to the dim surroundings, they heard a guttural growl echoing from within the depths of the warehouse.

"This way," Taryn muttered, motioning for Cierra to follow.

Turning several corners, they soon found themselves faced with a pack of mutants, each of them unsightly and hungry for blood.

A mutant lunged at Cierra. She sidestepped its attack, fluidly slicing her twin blades through the air and severing one of the creature's arms at the elbow. The beast howled in pain, but the sound was quickly drowned out by the cacophony of snarls and growls echoing all around.

There's so many of them!

"Behind you!" Taryn shouted, her voice carrying a razor-sharp edge of alarm.

Feeling a rush of air, Cierra instinctively ducked down as something narrowly missed her head. She then spun around to deliver a vicious kick to the mutant's misshapen face.

"Thanks, Taryn," Cierra said with a grunt, her mind racing as she tried to anticipate the next mutant.

She moved quickly to deflect another mutant's strike, her white hair whipping around like a ghostly halo. She gritted her teeth, feeling the strain in her muscles and the adrenaline pumping through her veins. Her breath came in ragged gasps, her lungs burning with each inhale.

Cierra and Taryn fought with every ounce of strength they had. The dire situation challenged them to their core, but they were ruthlessly driven in their plan to take down the enemy and protect the people of Willowbrook.

Confident that Taryn could keep the remaining mutants occupied, Cierra strategically edged herself away, approaching the surrounding doors and ground-floor windows.

She began to secure heavy iron bars across every possible exit available to the mutants, thankful that whoever had abandoned the warehouse hadn't bothered to clear it out. As she worked, the din of battle echoed around her. It was a symphony of chaos, driving her on.

Struggling to wedge a bar into a particularly stubborn door crevice, Cierra grunted under her breath. After exerting herself more than she'd had to with the other doors, finally, the bar slid into place with a satisfying *thunk*. Cierra allowed herself a small, grim smile. They were now another step closer to ending this nightmare.

"Almost there!" she called out to Taryn, who was skilfully holding her own against the relentless onslaught of mutants.

There's no way the mutants will have the leverage or tools to break through these barricades.

With every ground-floor window and door secured, Cierra joined Taryn in the fray, her twin blades slicing through the air with deadly precision. It pleased her to think that soon, every last one of these mutants would be trapped like rats in a cage.

"It's almost time," she shouted across to Taryn. "I'll get things cooking."

Darting away from the horde of mutants, who were all focused on Taryn, Cierra grabbed a piece of wood from the ground. Taking a box of matches from one of her pockets, she struck a light with confidence and placed the flickering ember to lick at the wood.

Placing the wood down and leaving the flames to hungrily consume it, Cierra moved to put herself in Taryn's line of sight, gesturing to her fellow assassin that it was now time to leave.

Fuelled by sheer adrenalin, the pair sprinted through the warehouse. As they passed stacks of decaying wood and forgotten furniture, they set them alight, turning the building into the beginnings of a blazing inferno.

As they neared a pile of broken furniture beneath a high window on the second floor, Cierra pulled several smoke bombs from her pocket. She glanced at Taryn, her eyes reflecting the ferocity of the flames around them.

Using the wreckage of tables and loose chair legs as footholds, they ascended the mound with ease. At the apex of the pile, now level with the window, Cierra could see the moonlight filtering in through the dusty glass. Relief flooded through her when she was able to open it, causing a reassuring breeze to invigorate her senses.

Perched together on the large windowsill, they hurled smoke bombs back into the warehouse. The explosions made an ear-shattering noise, releasing smoke, and vitally, chemicals that would fuel the fire's rapid spread.

"Go, go, go!" Cierra yelled.

They climbed out of the window and leapt like nimble felines onto the cobblestone street, coughing from the smoke that clung to them. Despite the lingering fear and exhaustion that weighed on them though, there was a shared sense of achievement.

Ensuring to distance themselves from the burning warehouse, they sprinted away, flames licking at the night sky behind them as the building succumbed to the blaze.

Epilogue

As the flames consumed the abandoned warehouse, obliterating the mutants and their nefarious plans, Cierra and Taryn made sure to get away from the scene unnoticed.

Awakened by the overbearing smoke as it made its way through the town, as dawn broke, the people of Willowbrook rallied together to combat the raging fire, armed with basic tools, but sheer determination. With grit and resolve, they aided the fire brigade in dousing the flames, extinguishing the blaze before it could spread further.

In the days that followed, word of Lady Blanch's demise spread quickly, bringing a sense of relief and closure to everyone in Willowbrook. Debts owed to the tyrant were forgotten. As for her guards and hangers-on, everyone was happy to disperse and move on to pastures new; no longer were they under the threatening thumb of the corrupt mutant woman.

Despite feeling proud of how they had succeeded to protect Willowbrook and its people, Cierra and Taryn were happy to remain anonymous, adamant in keeping their identities undisclosed. Although Violet had learnt firsthand of Cierra and Taryn's roles as assassins and had paid witness to their recent activities, she would forever honour her promise to keep it a secret.

Satisfied that her work in Willowbrook was done, Taryn bid farewell to Cierra and Violet, determined to work alone and take her skills to other people and places that may need her.

Happy and welcome to keep living with Violet, Cierra continued to work as an assassin under the cover of darkness. Although Willowbrook was safe for now, she knew that her services would most likely be needed in the future. With a steely resolve and unwavering dedication, she remained vigilant, ready to confront whatever dangers may await her in the never-ending quest for justice.

www.ingramcontent.com/pod-product-compliance
Lightning Source LLC
Chambersburg PA
CBHW061455210726
48287CB00007B/2519